THE ADVENTURES OF THUMBS UP JOHNNIE!®"

JOHNNIE FINDS A BUDDY©

www.thumbsupjohnnie.com

This book is dedicated to my four favorite friends: E.F. Bain, Darlene Bain, C.R. Sanders and Crystal Sanders. Their love and encouragement has always gone beyond grandparenting and led me to believe that I could attempt anything!

A special thank you to Mark Homyk & Heidi Huettner for their support & contributions.

Michelle Bain

$\mathcal{T}$humbs Up Johnnie is a happy little thumbprint with a good life and comfortable cowboy boots! He is a sweet fellow who loves working at his restaurant where he greets the hungry folks at the Longhorn Diner. He flips the "biggest flapjacks this side of the Texas border."

Johnnie loves his life in Happy, Texas, where he visits all of his friends at Lone Star Row, the main street in his friendly hometown. This is where all of the townspeople shop and greet one another with a friendly tip of their hats and a "Howdy, hello!"

$\mathcal{T}$oday Johnnie spent all morning flipping flapjacks. Afterwards he decided to visit one of his favorite stores on Lone Star Row, a place called Dime Store Sam's.

Johnnie loves Dime Store Sam's, it's the best place to shop in Happy, Texas. Sam has all the fun stuff! Last time he was there Johnnie bought a new kite, a glow-in-the dark yo-yo and his prized possession, a lucky lasso.

 4

"Hello, Dime Store Sam! How's the day treating you?" asked Johnnie.

"Fine and dandy!" said Dime Store Sam with his hundred-dollar smile. "The sun's a-shinin' and I got a new shipment of licorice bits and sour gum pops today. How about a taste?"

"I'm always up for a sweet treat. Thank you very much!" said Johnnie as he collected his bag of goodies, gave Sam a "thumbs up" and waved goodbye.

6

Johnnie skipped down Lone Star Row to see Banker Bill at Lucky Horseshoe Bank. He saved some money from flipping flapjacks and wanted to put it in his savings account.

"Good afternoon, Banker Bill! I'd like to make a deposit." said Johnnie, handing Bill a bag of money.

"That's wonderful! A dollar saved is a dollar earned, Johnnie," said Bill.

"By the way, those special silver dollar flapjacks were delicious this morning. A good breakfast sure helps me concentrate when I'm countin' money here at the bank!" said Bill.

"Well, I'm glad you liked 'em, Bill!" said Johnnie.

After Banker Bill deposited the money he handed Johnnie a little surprise. "Lucky Horse Shoe Bank is fifty years old today," said Bill. "To celebrate, we're giving each of our loyal customers a set of lucky horseshoes."

Johnnie was so thankful for the horseshoes that he felt a tickle in his stomach as he thought to himself, "What am I going to do with such a wonderful gift?"

"Thank you, Banker Bill!" said Johnnie as he waved goodbye and gave him a "thumbs up."

$\mathcal{T}$humbs Up Johnnie's next stop was the Rumblin' Tummy Bakery. He loves it there because they have the best cookies in Happy, Texas. Cookies are Johnnie's favorite treat! He's best friends with the owner, Lillian Pinky. Johnnie calls her "L'il Pinky" for short.

"Howdy, L'il Pinky!" said Johnnie as he walked through the bakery door. "My goodness, it smells yummy in here! What's baking today?" Johnnie asked.

11

"Well Johnnie, I'm baking molasses pie, oatmeal cookies, and red velvet cake today!" said L'il Pinky. "Would you like a cookie?"

"Yes I would! I can't resist anything in your bakery," said Thumbs Up Johnnie, giggling. "I've had a great day today, L'il. I got some free candy from Dime Store Sam, lucky horseshoes from Banker Bill and now a yummy treat from you!"

14

L'il Pinky smiled at Thumbs Up Johnnie and said, "Sounds like it is your lucky day! Tell me what you plan to do with those horseshoes from Banker Bill."

"Well, I reckon' I could hang them above my doorway for good luck!" replied Johnnie.

"Hey, I have an idea," said L'il Pinky. "Your boots are gettin' worn from walkin' back and forth to the diner every day. What about gettin' a horse to ride to work so you don't have to walk? Then you could save your energy for cooking flapjacks."

*J*ohnnie realized why he liked L'il Pinky so much- because she was always thinking. He thought to himself:

~ My boots are getting' worn!

~ I've always wanted a horse!

~ I have four brand new horseshoes!

~ Why not?

"That's a great idea! But where would I get a horse?" asked Johnnie.

L'il Pinky grinned with delight as she sliced Johnnie a big piece of warm molasses pie and said, "My uncle has a beautiful horse ranch over in Spur, Texas. I reckon you could find a horse there, Johnnie."

Johnnie was so excited about going to a horse ranch that he shouted with excitement, "Can we go tomorrow?"

L'il Pinky arranged with her uncle to visit the ranch the next day to pick out a horse for Johnnie.

"Tomorrow I'll have a horse of my very own!" thought Johnnie.

Thumbs Up Johnnie was so excited he could hardly sleep that night! It was just like the day he bought his first cowboy hat and boots. He slept with one eye open, waiting for the sun to come up.

By the next morning, Johnnie was excited as ever to hear L'il Pinky knock on his front door. He ran to the door, almost slipping out of his boots. "Hello, L'il! I'm really for our trip to Tumbleweed Ranch. Are you?" asked Johnnie.

"Yes, I'm ready to go. I packed some goodies from the bakery so we won't get hungry on our trip! I also grabbed some carrots to feed to the horses. Now let's go find you a horse, Johnnie!" said L'il Pinky.

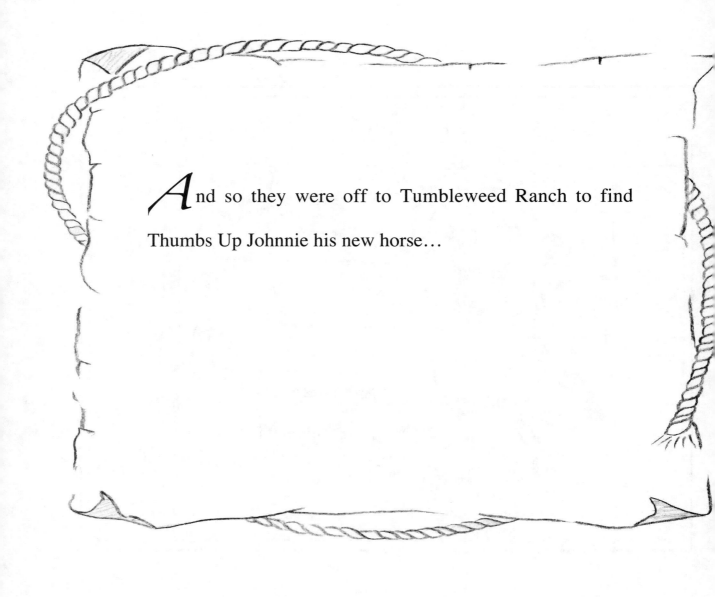

*A*nd so they were off to Tumbleweed Ranch to find

Thumbs Up Johnnie his new horse…

25

26

"Wow! Tumbleweed Ranch is really beautiful." Johnnie said with excitement. "I bet the perfect horse for me lives here."

"Oh, yes, I think so," said L'il Pinky. "My uncle loves horses and takes tender-loving care of them!"

Thumbs Up Johnnie was so excited he was shaking in his boots. He couldn't wait to get to the barn!

"*H*owdy!" a booming voice hollered from the corral. L'il Pinky recognized it immediately as Uncle Bob.

"Bronco Bob" (as his friends called him) had worked with horses all his life. He knew each horse had its own personality, a "special something" that made each one unique.

"I have a lot of good horses in the barn, Johnnie," said Bronco Bob. "Let's take a look inside - I'm sure we'll find you one."

Thumbs Up Johnnie and L'il Pinky walked through the barn and fed carrots to the horses. They were good horses, just as Bronco Bob said. They all looked happy and content. Johnnie loved them all!

*I*n one stall, though, they noticed a little horse standing in the corner and looking very sad.

"What about this little guy, Uncle Bob? He looks sad, like he lost his best friend," said L'il Pinky.

"Poor little fella. He's lonely," Bronco Bob replied. "His sister left two weeks ago to live with a young girl. A week later, his best friend went to go live at the farm next door. They were really close and now they only get to see each other every once in while."

34

Bronco Bob opened up the stall and said in a gentle voice, "Hey, boy…don't be so sad. Cheer up! My niece and her friend want to give you a treat. Come on, boy, turn around and meet 'em."

Slowly, the horse turned around and looked up at Thumbs Up Johnnie and L'il Pinky. He blinked very slowly, as if to say, "Howdy!"

Thumbs Up Johnnie asked Bronco Bob, "What's the little fella's name?"

36

*B*ronco Bob replied, "His name is Buddy. Watch this…"

Slowly, Bronco Bob took the bridle and led the horse towards L'il Pinky and Johnnie. L'il Pinky walked towards Buddy and put a carrot underneath his nose. Buddy looked at her with his big, brown, mopey eyes and blinked very slowly, as if to say, "Thank you, Ma'am!"

Buddy knew just by looking at L'il Pinky that she was nice. He also smelled her freshly baked muffins in the picnic basket a few feet from the stall and hoped she would feed him one of those!

*N*ext, Thumbs Up Johnnie walked up to Buddy and slowly put his hand under Buddy's nose. Buddy twitched his freckly, pink nose and made a loud "neigh." It almost sounded like "Hello." Johnnie began gently scratching Buddy's nose and tickling his whiskers. Buddy inched closer to Thumbs Up Johnnie to make sure he didn't stop that good scratching! The two were instant pals.

*B*ronco Bob was pleased that Buddy was happy. He hadn't seen him like that in a long time. "Do you like the little fella?" asked Bob.

Thumbs Up Johnnie replied, "Sure do! He's just as sweet as molasses. I know the kind of nose scratching he loves. Bronco Bob, I would really like to take Buddy home to my ranch."

"Sure," Bronco Bob replied, "I would love for you to take Buddy home, but you have to pledge to always take care of him."

They had found the perfect horse! L'il Pinky and Thumbs Up Johnnie packed up their basket and put a blanket and saddle on Buddy. Johnnie hopped up onto Buddy and gave a "thumbs up " while thanking Bronco Bob.

"Goodbye," said Bronco Bob.

Thumbs Up Johnnie was glad he could give his new "Buddy" a home. "Hmmm, I wonder if he likes flapjacks," he thought.

It was one of the best days of Johnnie's life! He spent the entire day with his best friend, L'il Pinky. And he knew that his new pal, Buddy, would be the perfect horse for him.

As the three of them walked back home through Bluebonnet Pasture Johnnie was so excited he felt butterflies in his stomach. He was sure that many fun adventures with his friends were just about to begin.

46